For Stella, Merry Christmas!
2012 2011

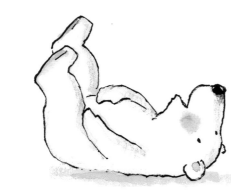

D0475138

For You

tiger tales

an imprint of ME Media, LLC

202 Old Ridgefield Road, Wilton, CT 06897

Published in the United States 2004

Originally published as *Omdat ik zoveel van je hou* in Belgium 2003

By Uitgeverij Clavis, Amersterdam-Hasselt

Copyright ©2003 Uitgeverij Clavis, Amersterdam-Hasselt

CIP data is available

ISBN 1-58925-039-7

Printed in China

All rights reserved

3 5 7 9 10 8 6 4 2

Library of Congress Cataloging-in-Publication Data

Genechten, Guido van.
  [Omdat ik zoveel van je hou. English]
  Because I love you so much / by Guido van Genechten.
      p. cm.
Summary: Although Snowy the polar bear asks his mother many questions,
he already knows many things, including the fact that his mother loves
him very much.
  ISBN 1-58925-039-7 (Hardcover)
  [1. Mother and child—Fiction. 2. Polar bear—Fiction. 3.
Bears—Fiction.] I. Title.
PZ7.G2912Be 2004
[E]—dc22
                                                        2003019308

Because I Love You So Much

by Guido van Genechten

tiger tales

Snowy was a very smart bear.
He knew where to find the best fish,
and he knew how to catch them.

He knew how to catch the biggest snowflakes, and he knew how to catch the best-tasting ones, too.

Snowy knew how cold the wind could be,
and he knew which way it blew.

He knew how to climb up an iceberg,
and how to slide down one, too.

Snowy knew how strong or weak the
ice could be, and he knew that when it
cracked it separated him from Mommy.

He knew that the sun only shone during the day, and that the moon only came out at night.

Snowy knew all these things,
and more. But there were some
things that he didn't understand.

"Where does snow come from, Mommy?"

"Well, you see Snowy," Mommy began, "very far from here the sun warms up the sea. Millions of water drops float up from the sea and gather together to become a cloud. Then the wind blows that cloud all the way over here. Because it's so cold here, the cloud begins to shiver. And when the cloud shakes, it snows!"

"But why is snow pure white, when the sea is so blue?"

That was a harder question, and Mommy wasn't sure of the answer. "Hmm," she said. "Snow is always white, just like polar bears are always white."

"And why are polar bears always white?" Snowy asked.

"Because white is the brightest, prettiest, sweetest, most beautiful color for a polar bear!" Mommy said proudly.

Snowy thought about this for a moment. "If I were yellow," Snowy asked, "would you still think I was pretty and sweet?"

"Of course!" Mommy said.

"And if I were red or green or blue all over, would you still think I was beautiful and bright?"

"Sure I would!" Mommy smiled.

"But why?" Snowy asked.

"Because I love

you so much!"
said Mommy.

And that was something Snowy
already knew.